IS FOR AMBER

PAULA DANZIGER

GET READY FOR SECOND GRADE, AMBER BROWN

Illustrated by Tony Ross

Hodder
Children's
Books

a division of Hodder Headline Limited

Much thanks to
Sheryl Hardin and her Brainy Bunch at
Gullett Elementary School 2000-2001:
Jacob Backhaus
Ashley Calhoun
Amber Day
Neal Edmondson
Kelly Ellis
Gregory Gomez
Will Grover
Danielle Johnson
Kramer Jones
Alex Manulik
Frances Mayo
Simon McCann
Jordyn Michalik
Madalyn Montgomery
Kristin Page
Kate Van Dyke
Victor Vogt
Kelly Wray

Text copyright © 2002 by Paula Danziger
Illustrations copyright © 2002 by Tony Ross
The right of Paula Danziger to be identified as the Author
and Tony Ross as the Illustrator of the Work has been asserted by them
in accordance with the Copyright, Designs and Patents Act 1988.
First published in 2002 by G.P. Putnam's Sons,
a division of Penguin Putnam Books for Young Readers,
345 Hudson Street, New York, NY 10014.
This paperback edition first published in the UK, in 2002 by Hodder Children's Books,
a division of Hodder Headline Limited,
338 Euston Road, London NW1 3BH

10 9 8 7 6 5 4 3 2 1

ISBN 0 340 84153 2

To the Salwens –

Peter, Peggy, James and William –

with love – P.D.

The good news is that I, Amber Brown,

am going to be a second-grader.

The bad news is that Mrs Wilson,

the second-grade teacher,

had to quit two weeks ago.

Her husband got a new job and they moved.

Anyone who was ever a second-grader

LOVED Mrs Wilson

and said she was a great teacher.

She used to smile at me in the hall.

Now there's going to be a new teacher.

I don't know her.

She doesn't know me.

What if she doesn't like me?

I try not to think about it.

In just one hour I will find out

who the second-grade teacher is.

Right now I will get ready for school.

On my bed are all my school supplies:

new pens and pencils, a new notebook,

and my lucky pen with purple feathers.

I unzip my new teddy-bear backpack.

My aunt Pam sent it to me.

She said that it's an "Enjoy Second Grade
Present".

I named him Bear Lee.

His full name is Bear Lee Brown

because he is barely brown,

and he is barely ready for second grade.

Just like me.

I put everything in my backpack and zip it up.

"Bear Lee," I say, "you are so special.

Everyone is going to like you

except Hannah Burton.

But don't worry. She is mean to

a lot of people, especially me."

"Amber," my mom calls upstairs.

"It's time for breakfast."

I pick up Bear Lee and look in the mirror.

I'm wearing my new clothes.

On my knee is a scab.

It is almost ready to fall off.

I named it Scabulous.

Bear Lee, Scabulous, and I are ready.

Second grade, here we come!

Breakfast.

Mom and Dad have breakfast with me.

"You look beautiful," Dad says.

I smile at him.

"You look clever,"

he continues.

"You look like everybody

will want you to be their best friend."

Mom puts a bowl of cereal in front of me.

"I know that this is going to be

a great year for you," she says.

I, Amber Brown, know

that they are just saying that

because they are my mom and dad.

We finish our breakfast.

There's a knock on the door.

It's Justin, my best friend from next door.

He is wearing his new Roboman backpack.

My dad is driving Justin and me to school.

Justin says, "This year

I am going to tell chicken jokes."

I just look at him.

"Why did the chicken

cross the playground?" he asks.

I think about it. "To get to second grade?"

He makes a face. "No, silly.

To get to the other slide."

My father laughs and so do I.

We get out of the car and go to the playground.

That's where second-graders meet

before school starts.

Jimmy Russell and Bobby Clifford

are wrestling on the ground

in their brand-new school clothes.

Vinnie Simmons is showing everyone

the snake tattoo on his arm.

Even though he tells everyone it is real,

I can tell that it's not.

I stick my finger in my mouth to get it wet.

I ask Vinnie to let me look at the tattoo.

I touch it with my wet finger.

Some of it comes off.

I don't say anything, but I, Amber Brown,

know for sure that the tattoo is not

on Vinnie's arm forever.

Vinnie knows I know.

He sticks out his tongue at me.

Gregory Gifford and Freddie Romano

are showing each other the tricks

that they have learned over the summer.

Gregory can whistle, standing on his hands.

Freddie can recite fifteen state capitals

and do armpit music at the same time.

The girls are talking about the new teacher.

Alicia Sanchez says her name is Ms
Light.

"I hear that she really wants to teach
high school students," Alicia says.

"I hear that she calls second-graders
'knee biters'," Naomi Schwartz adds.

Tiffany Schroeder holds on to
her good-luck Barbie doll.

"I'm scared," she says.

"I want Mrs Wilson to come back."

Hannah Burton joins our group.

She looks at my backpack.

"How baby, Amber. A second-grader

shouldn't wear a baby backpack

that looks like a teddy bear."

I am not going to let Hannah

ruin second grade for me.

I ignore Hannah Burton.

Naomi and Alicia put their animal backpacks

down next to Bear Lee and look at Hannah.

She shrugs and mumbles, "Babies."

My class talks about Ms Light

and the things that we are worried about.

I wasn't so worried until we all started talking.

What if she gives seven hours of homework?

What if she gets really upset

if we colour outside the lines?

What if she doesn't give out bathroom passes?

What if she's an alien from some foreign planet?

The bell rings.

It's time to meet Ms Light.

We all go inside to Room 2.

Ms Light is waiting for us at the door.

She doesn't look like any teacher

I've ever seen before.

She looks like a high school kid

or a baby-sitter.

She's wearing a denim dress.

There are all sorts of patches and pins on it –

school buses, pens, pencils,

chalkboards, chalk, books, paper…

And she's got on earrings

that are shaped like lightbulbs…

and they light up.

I get it… Ms Light.

Lightbulbs.

She smiles and says
"Hello" and "Welcome"
to each of us as we go in.
She even says hello to Bear Lee.
I'm beginning to think
that Ms Light might be okay.

The entire room is decorated.

We go to the seats

where our names are written

on cardboard cutouts of lightbulbs.

I'm sitting with Fredrich Allen.

I hope that over the summer

he stopped picking his nose.

I'm sitting with Justin Daniels.

Hooray.

I'm sitting with Hannah Burton.

Yuck.

Hannah looks at my name

on the cardboard lightbulb.

"Amber Brown. What a sap you are.

Ugh. You probably don't even know

that amber comes from tree sap that gets hard.

Sometimes there are things

like spiders and bugs in it."

I know she is right about that.

My mom gave me a book about amber,

and my dad gave me an amber pendant

with a little fly in it.

Hannah makes a face at me.

That's it.

I say, "Look, Hannah BURPton. Stop it."

Fredrich Allen says,

"Hannah Burpton."

Justin starts singing,

"Unhappy Burpton to you."

Ms Light stands at the front of the room.

"Welcome to second grade,"

she says, and smiles at us.

"This is going to be such

an exciting school year.

We are going to learn new things

about the world and ourselves."

She continues,

"As you know, my name is Ms Light.

Do you know what the word 'light' means?"

I raise my hand quickly.

I want to be the first person

to answer a question in second grade.

Everyone else has a hand raised.

Ms Light chooses Fredrich.

"Light is a kind of energy," he says.

Fredrich Allen is very smart.

Ms Light beams at him.

I guess that makes it a Light beam.

She says, "Absolutely right.

Light helps us to see things.

Most of our light comes from the sun.

Some of our light comes from the moon.

We get light from electricity

when we flick a switch."

Justin pretends to put his finger

in a make-believe socket.

"ZZZZZZZZZZZing."

Ms Light nods at him.

"That can really happen…

Electricity can be very powerful."

"Wow," we all say.

She grins at me. "Amber. Do you know

what your name has to do

with the word 'electricity'?"

I shake my head no.

She continues,

"The word 'electricity' comes

from the word 'electron'.

Electricity is flowing electrons.

The Greek word for 'electron' is…"

Everyone looks at me.

"Amber," Ms Light says.

I light up.

I, Amber Brown, am so happy.

I guess now that I know about electricity,

I can say that I am all charged up.

Turning to Justin, I grin.

He gives me a thumbs-up. "Way to go."

I look at Hannah Burton.

I smile and cross my eyes.

Ms Light continues,

"I want all of you to have lots of energy

to learn and to grow.

I, Ms Light, want to help you

shine as students.

"From now on," she says,

"you are going to be the group

known as the Bright Lights."

We all grin.

Next, Ms Light gives us all of the rules
we will follow in second grade.

We will be respectful.

We will be on time.

We will do our work.

Then she picks up a book from her desk

and goes to her rocking chair.

She starts reading us a book.

It's a story book. Hooray!

By the end of the year,

I, Amber Brown, am going to be able

to read a story book all on my own.

And next year, when I go to third grade,

I'm going to tell the new second-graders

that they don't have to be scared.

I, Amber Brown,

am ready for second grade.